HOT WHEELS™

Racing U.S.A.

By Myles Ryder

Illustrated by Dave White

SCHOLASTIC INC.

New York   Toronto   London   Auckland   Sydney
Mexico City   New Delhi   Hong Kong   Buenos Aires

ISBN-13: 978-0-545-08505-2
ISBN-10: 0-545-08505-5

12 11 10 9   15 16 17/0

Printed in the U.S.A.   40
First printing, September 2008

Today is the big
race across the U.S.A.

The cars line up. The engines roar.

The fog lifts. Ready, set, RACE!

Golden Gate Bridge, California

The red car takes an early lead.

Monument Valley, Utah

The road is dry. The sun is hot.

The yellow car needs more gas.

Look out for snakes!

Grand Canyon, Arizona

7

The cars are riding high.
The drivers do not look down.

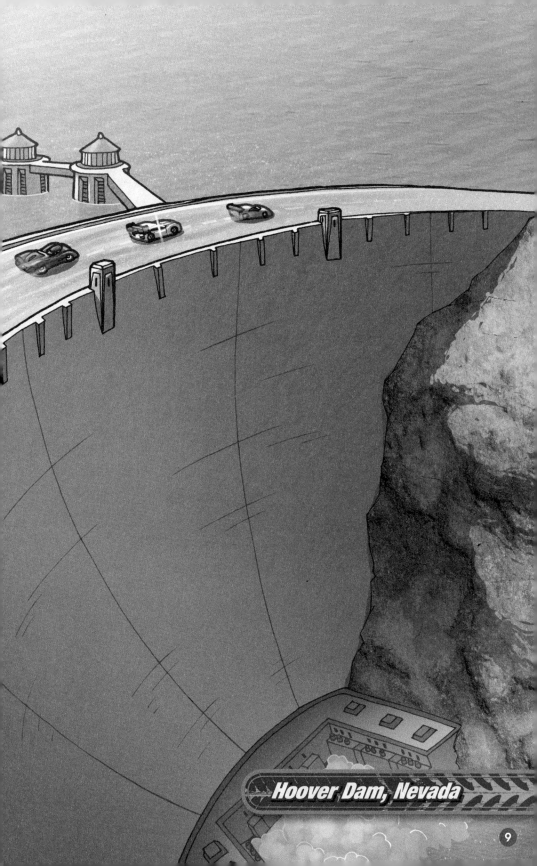

Hoover Dam, Nevada

Some roads are smooth.
Some roads are bumpy.

Look at the
faces in the rock!

It is raining hard.
The blue car skids.
Water rises in the river.
The white car is stuck.

The cars zoom like rockets.

Get ready to blast off!

Cape Canaveral, Florida

The cars go over the hills.
Is that a bear?

The green car is in front.

Horses have their own race.
Who is faster?
The car or the horse?

Welcome to the capital city!
The cherry trees are in bloom.

Look at that sight.

And listen to that waterfall!

Niagara Falls, New York

The coast is rocky.
The ocean looks cold.

LOBSTER

The orange car
passes the black car.

Its engine makes a noise.

Oh, no! The orange car
spins off the road.

The black car blows a tire.
The blue car moves ahead.

Welcome to New York City.
We have a winner!

HOT WHEELS™

New York City, New York